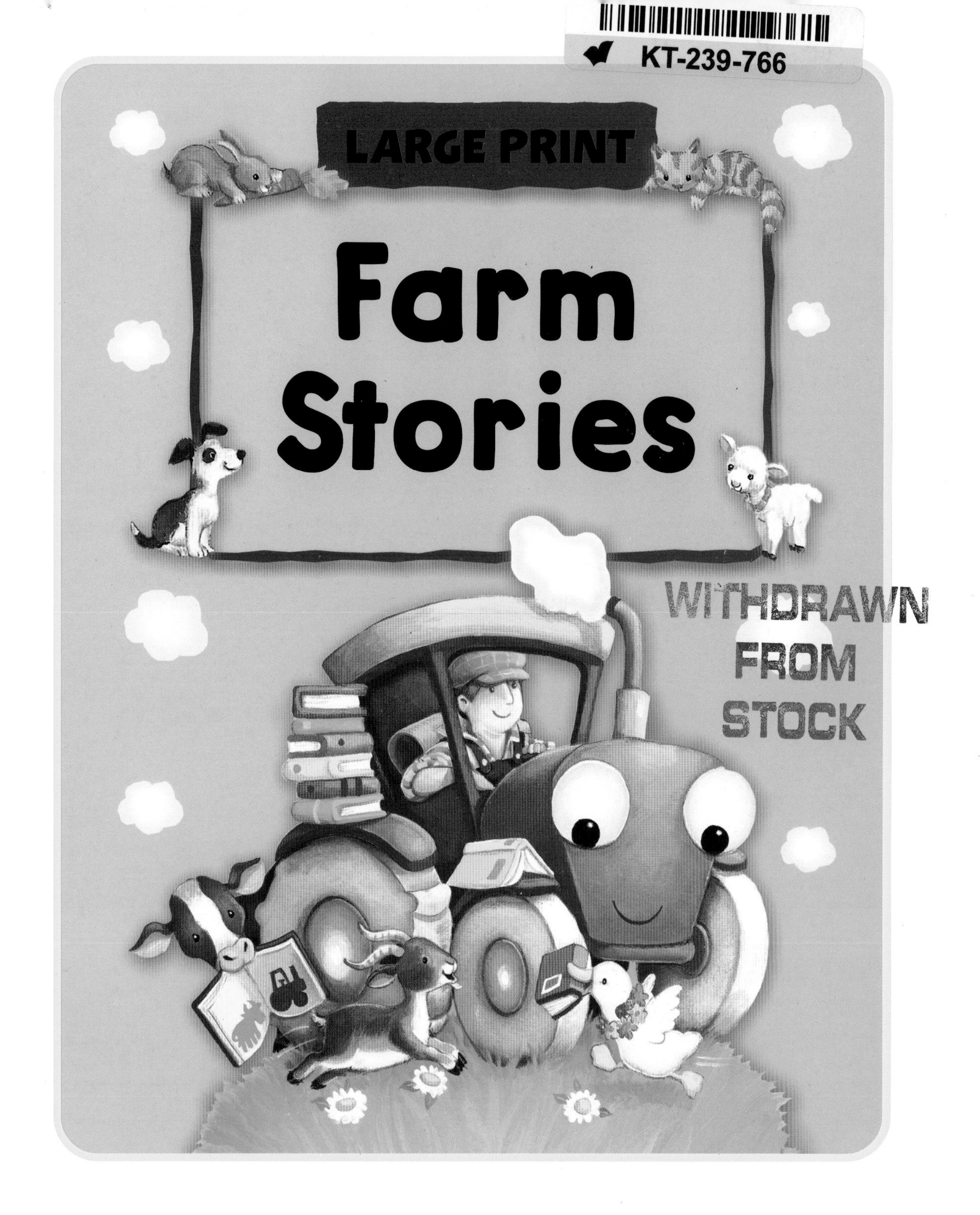

ENGLAND

Cloud Spotting

Farmer Chris is cloud spotting. “Look!” he says, pointing to the sky. “That cloud looks just the same shape as a tractor!”

Billy Goat and Princess the pony join in. Billy can definitely see a cloud that is shaped like a carrot. "This is fun!" neighs Princess.

Marmalade the cat opens one eye to see what is going on. All of the animals are gazing into the blue sky, shouting out shapes they can see in the clouds.

Even Oscar the owl wakes up from his daytime sleep. “I was dreaming about mice, and now I can see them!” he hoots.

Then they see a cloud that looks like a clover leaf. "Look!" they shout. "Where is Clover the cow? She has a cloud especially for her!" But Clover isn't there.

Finally, they find Clover standing at the top of a hill. "What are you doing?" they ask her.

"I wanted to get a better view of the clouds," she says. "So I thought I would climb a little bit closer to the sky." Silly old Clover!

A Special Surprise

Something very strange has happened in the barn. Harriet the hen has laid five eggs, and one of them is pink! All of the animals are surprised. Harriet is extremely shocked! How did that happen?

Rocky Rooster wants to spread the news. “Cock-a-doodle-come to the barn!” he crows. Camilla the cow asks what is going on. “Harriet has laid a pink egg!” says Rocky. “Come and see!”

Harriet sits patiently on her eggs to keep them warm. Every time she climbs off to look, she wonders how one of them turned out pink. She hears a cracking noise and knows that the eggs are about to hatch.

“Come quickly!” crows Rocky. Little Parkin Pig is rolling in the mud. He doesn’t know about the pink egg. Rocky tells him, and says the eggs are hatching. Parkin jumps up and runs to the barn.

When they arrive at the barn, guess what they see? The eggs have all hatched, and Harriet has five new chicks. One of them is bright pink, with yellow spots and green legs. How did that happen?

Oscar Owl is very wise, and has seen many things. He has never seen a pink chick, though! Soon, all the animals have heard about Harriet's special baby.

When the farmer sees the pink chick, he scratches his head. "Well, now," he says. "What have we here? And what will people think? Most unusual indeed. I've never seen anything like it!"

The farmer's children love the new chick. They call her Perky, and help Harriet to look after her. When she is big enough, they take her to the village fair. Of course, everyone is surprised to see her. She is so special that she wins first prize in the Best Chicks competition. Well done, Perky!

1

Super Skaters

This year's freezing weather has arrived at Rosehip Farm. The tractor is locked in the barn, and Farmer Chris stays in the farmhouse to do his paperwork.

Many of the animals stay indoors, too. It is so cold outside! But Gabby Goose loves the frosty mornings and the twinkling white landscape. “Come along, my lovelies!’ she says. “It’s skating season!”

Gabby is going to the farm pond with her ice skates. It is so cold that the water has frozen solid. “Are you coming, little chicks?” she asks, on her way past the hen house.

"We can't come skating," cry the chicks. "We don't have any skates. Mummy says there are too many of us, and our feet are growing too fast."

Gabby is sad that the chicks can't join in the fun. There are so many of her friends skating around on the ice. Then she sees Terry Toad, who is practising fancy tricks on his skates.

She looks across the pond and sees all of Terry's brothers and sisters. They are very good at skating and zoom around at top speed. They have been learning to skate since they were tiny toads.

Gabby has an idea. She visits Mrs Toad to ask for her help. "Of course!" croaks Mrs Toad. "I have lots of pairs of little skates. My children are too big for these now."

Soon, the little chicks are trying out their new skates. Charlie and Cherry get the hang of it straight away, but little Chico is finding it hard. “I guess I need to practise some more,” he chirps. “but this is FUN!”

Lost and Found

Pebbles the puppy is in a playful mood. He wants to play with his favourite blue bone. Where can it be?

Pebbles looks for the bone in his basket. He searches under the cushion, and in all of the blankets. It isn't there!

Pebbles asks the sheepdog puppies if they have seen his bone. “We haven’t seen your blue bone,” they bark. “But we have lots of other bones and toys. You can share those with us if you like!”

It is very kind of them, but Pebbles really wants to find his best blue bone. He decides to keep on looking.

Pebbles runs out into the farmyard. Maybe he left his bone out there? "Have you seen my bone?" he asks the hens in the hen house. They look, but can't find it anywhere.

Scruffy Scarecrow sees Pebbles looking sad, and asks what is wrong. He hasn't seen the bone either, but he wants to help. He calls the farm animals together.

Lots of animals turn up to try to help Pebbles. They can see how sad he is. “Think about the last place you played with it,” suggests Gussie Goose. “It might still be there.”

Pebbles thinks hard. Then he has an idea. “I was lying by the fire to keep warm,” he says. “And chewing on my best blue bone.” He rushes into the farmhouse – and there is his bone, with the firewood. Now he is a very happy pup!

A Busy Day

Hoppy Bunny is racing around. She looks very busy indeed. "What are you doing?" ask her friends. "No time to talk!" she shouts, and hops off at top speed.

She zooms past a bumblebee collecting pollen. “You look as busy as me!” he buzzes. “What are you doing?” Hoppy Bunny stops just long enough to say, “I’m busier than a busy bee!” and then runs off.

The ducks on the pond see Hoppy Bunny running past. "What are you doing?" they quack. "No time to talk!" pants Hoppy Bunny. "I'm too busy!"

Hoppy Bunny runs to the milking shed. All of the cows are queuing to be milked. “Aren’t you busy?” asks Hoppy Bunny. The cows explain that they have to wait patiently.

Inside the milking shed, Hoppy Bunny can see how busy it is. The cows just stand there, but Farmer Chris has to work very fast to milk them all. "He's as busy as I am!" thinks Hoppy Bunny.

Hoppy Bunny rushes on. She must get to the fields where Red Tractor is ploughing. "He's so busy!" she says to the birds overhead. They agree with her, and watch as she hops all around the field.

Finally, Hoppy Bunny returns home. She looks so tired. “What ARE you doing?” ask her friends. “Well, I’m being busy!” says Hoppy Bunny. “Isn’t everyone on a farm supposed to be busy?”

Her friends all smile. “You are a funny bunny! All the busy people are doing jobs – not just being busy! Now it looks like you could do with a rest...” but before they have finished, Hoppy Bunny is fast asleep. She’s had a busy day!

A Really Bad Cold

Daddy Duck has a cold. He can't stop sneezing.

"Aaachoo!" he blasts.
"Aaaaaaaaaachoo. AAAACHOO!"

Poor Daddy Duck! He sneezes so hard that he rocks all of the lily pads in the pond. Felicity Frog is NOT happy to be knocked off her leaf.

Daddy Duck sneezes so hard that he blasts a dragonfly straight at Tony Toad. The big old toad is NOT happy to be hit on the head by an insect.

The pond animals want Daddy Duck to go away until he stops sneezing. "Something awful is going to happen if he stays in the pond," they say. Sure enough, Daddy Duck's next sneeze is so hard that Mindy Moorhen is blown right off her nest.

Daddy's sneeze makes a huge wave that washes across the pond. It is so big that his smallest duckling gets washed away into the reeds. She is only tiny and doesn't know how to get home.

The little duckling swims around until she hears cheeping noises. Is she home already? No – it's Mrs Swan and her cygnet babies. "How do I get home?" asks the little duckling. Mrs Swan points to the edge of the pond.

The little duckling waddles ashore. She can hear more cheeping noises. She climbs onto a pile of straw but only finds Mrs Turkey and her chicks. “How do I get home?” asks the little duckling. Mrs Turkey points to the yard.

In the yard, she hears cheeping noises again. She finds Mrs Hen and her chicks behind a large barrel. "How do I get home?" she asks. Mrs Hen shows her how to get back to the pond.

At the pond, the little duckling can hear cheeping noises, but she is scared it won't be the right family. Then she hears another sound. "Aaaaaaaaa-choo!" Quickly, she paddles across. Sure enough, her whole family is there to cuddle her.

"They warned your daddy that his sneezing was bad," quacks Mummy Duck. "Yes," says the little duckling, "but it was good as well. That's how I found you all again!" Daddy Duck laughs and laughs – and sneezes some more.

A Helping Hand

Rosie was a little piglet with a very curly tail. She was good friends with all the animals on the farm. One day, she squeezed through the fence to visit everyone she knew.

“Hello, Mrs Moo!” she said. “What are you doing today?” Mrs Moo was going to the milking shed. Rosie wanted to go, too. “Not today, Rosie,” said Mrs Moo. “There’s nothing for you to do there.”

Rosie ran towards the old windmill. The mice were sweeping up all the leaves that were blowing from the trees. "Can I help?" asked Rosie. "Thank you, but no," they squeaked. "We don't have another brush for you."

Poor Rosie felt a little bit sad. She went to the river to find Shadow, the goose. She was washing clothes. “Can I help?” asked Rosie. “Sorry, Rosie,” honked Shadow. “I’ve nearly finished.”

Little Rosie felt very sad now. Nobody wanted her help! She ran to the barn and hid in a pile of straw. Why wasn't there anything she could do for her friends?

Rosie's mum couldn't find her little piglet anywhere. She was worried about her. She asked Rosie's friends if they had seen her. Dandy Duck thought she had seen Rosie running into the barn.

Mrs Pig found Rosie in the barn and gave her a cuddle. “Come out here,” she said. “I need your help.” Rosie cheered up. “Do you want me to make the sandwiches for lunch?” she snorted.

"Well, noooo..." said her mum. Rosie stopped smiling. "Actually," said Mrs Pig, "it's a much nicer job than that. We want you to help us eat some of this food!" Rosie sat with her friends and they all ate a happy lunch together.

The Farmer Wins a Prize

Farmer Bob has bought a new tractor. "Look at it!" he says to his wife. "Look how shiny and red it is! I am going to enter it in the county show. I'm sure it will win a prize!"

The farmer can't stop looking at his new tractor. He even talks about it to the animals! "Oh, it's a lovely vehicle. My friend Farmer Joe will surely want one, when he sees it!"

Farmer Bob phones Farmer Joe to ask if he is entering the county show. "Erm, maybe," says Joe. "No – definitely! Of course I am. I'll see you there." Now Farmer Joe needs to find a vehicle. He looks outside in the old barn.

At the very back of the barn, hidden in a pile of junk, Farmer Joe finds what he is looking for. His trusty old horse-drawn carriage! It certainly needs some work, though. He finds his cleaning things, and lots of paint and brushes.

On the morning of the county show, Farmer Bob gets up early to wash his new red tractor. He gives it a final polish and stands back, smiling. "Such a beauty!" he smiles. "A certain prize winner!"

That same morning, Farmer Joe and his wife get up even earlier. They groom Cal the carthorse and braid his mane. They add flowers and bells to his reins so he jingles as he trots. He looks so smart!

When Cal is ready, Farmer Joe fetches the carriage. How different it looks! Joe has worked really hard. Now it is clean and bright, covered in shiny blue paint. "Come on, Cal," says Joe. "Time to go!"

Cal trots proudly to the showground pulling the carriage. Everyone smiles and waves. The judges are very impressed, and he wins first prize in the Best Vehicle competition. Farmer Bob's tractor is given second prize – so he did win something, after all!

Little Lost Lamb

Farmer Tim is working hard in the fields. There is lots of ploughing to be done on this sunny day. Little Blue Tractor is bored. He wishes there was something more exciting to do.

At the top of the hill, two sheep run up to Little Blue Tractor. "Heeeeelp!" they bleat. "Sally's lamb has gone missing. We can't find her anywhere!" Now Little Blue Tractor has an exciting job to do!

Little Blue Tractor drives around the farm. “Have you seen Sally’s lamb?” he asks Billy Goat. Billy has an idea. “There are lots of sheep in Farmer Ben’s field,” he bleats. “We should look there.”

They drive to Farmer Ben's field. But all of his sheep have been sheared. Sally's lamb would be easy to see, as she still has all of her curly white wool. Where should they look next?

Soon, they have looked all over. Little Blue Tractor drives back to the farmhouse. He passes a field where Charlie is playing on an old red tractor. His sister Layla is playing too – with Sally's lamb!

The little lamb had run away from the field and Layla had found her. "I was going to take her back soon," she says. "But she is so woolly and cuddly!" No one is cross with her, and everyone is pleased that Sally's lamb is safe. Now she has a new friend, too!

Food Glorious Food

It is Farmer Chris's birthday. Happy birthday, Chris! But as any farmer will tell you, there is lots of work to be done, even on such a special day. He still gets up when the sun rises, and works for hours before he takes a break.

When he has his cup of tea, his wife has a surprise for him. She has baked him a birthday cake. The sheepdog puppies hope that he might spare a slice for them.

Mrs Hen and her chicks don't like birthday cake. Instead, they celebrate the farmer's birthday with a nice slice of corn and worm pie.

Darcey the pony and her foal don't need cake. They have a whole field full of delicious grass to eat. Neigh...neigh... happy birthday from us!

The sneaky mice might have some cake when no one is looking...but for now, they have managed to find some delicious cheese to celebrate the farmer's birthday.